WELCOME TO
PASSPORT TO READING
A beginning reader's ticket to a brand-new world!

Every book in this program is designed to build read-along and read-alone skills, level by level, through engaging and enriching stories. As the reader turns each page, he or she will become more confident with new vocabulary, sight words, and comprehension.

These PASSPORT TO READING levels will help you choose the perfect book for every reader.

READING TOGETHER
Read short words in simple sentence structures together to begin a reader's journey.

READING OUT LOUD
Encourage developing readers to sound out words in more complex stories with simple vocabulary.

READING INDEPENDENTLY
Newly independent readers gain confidence reading more complex sentences with higher word counts.

READY TO READ MORE
Readers prepare for chapter books with fewer illustrations and longer paragraphs.

This book features sight words from the educator-supported Dolch Sight Words List. This encourages the reader to recognize commonly used vocabulary words, increasing reading speed and fluency.

Enjoy the journey!

ABDOPUBLISHING.COM

Reinforced library bound edition published in 2018 by Spotlight, a division of ABDO, PO Box 398166, Minneapolis, Minnesota 55439. Spotlight produces high-quality reinforced library bound editions for schools and libraries. Published by agreement with Little, Brown and Company.

Printed in the United States of America, North Mankato, Minnesota.
092017
012018

 THIS BOOK CONTAINS RECYCLED MATERIALS

LIBRARY OF CONGRESS CATALOGING-IN-PUBLICATION DATA

This book was previously cataloged with the following information:

Hughes, Emily C.
  Ponies love pets! / by Emily C. Hughes. — First edition.
    pages cm. — (My little pony) (Passport to reading. Level 1)
  ISBN 9780316368858 (pbk)
  I. Hughes, Emily C. Ponies love pets! II. Title.
  PZ7.H87314 Po 2014
  [E]—dc23
            2013027772

978-1-5321-4096-9 (Reinforced Library Bound Edition)

A Division of ABDO
abdopublishing.com

PONIES LOVE PETS!

by Emily C. Hughes

LITTLE, BROWN AND COMPANY
New York Boston

ABDO
Spotlight

Attention, My Little Pony fans!
Look for these items when you read this book.
Can you spot them all?

alligator

cattle

tortoise

phoenix

These ponies are best friends.

They love to laugh together.

They also love to play with their pets!

The ponies and their pets are
always there to help one another.

Angel is Fluttershy's pet bunny.

He can be a little bossy.

But Angel makes Fluttershy
feel better when she is sad.

Pinkie Pie has a pet alligator named Gummy.
Most ponies would not want an alligator
for a pet, but Gummy is special.
He has no teeth!

It is lucky because he LOVES to bite!

Twilight Sparkle has Owlowiscious.
He helps her by bringing books from
the library.

At first, he and Spike did not get along,
but now they are good friends.

15

A pony like Applejack needs
a good work dog like Winona!
Winona helps the Apple family
herd the cattle.

The Apple family got Winona

when she was a puppy.

She loves to run and leap and

have her belly scratched!

Rainbow Dash wants a pet as fast and cool as she is, like a falcon or a bat.

She has a contest to find the best animal.

Fluttershy has lots of ideas.

Soon Rainbow Dash meets Tank,
a tortoise who saves her
when a rock falls on her wing.

Tank may be slow,

but Rainbow Dash fixes that.

She turns him into a flying tortoise!

Opalescence is Rarity's cat.
She helps make beautiful
dresses for the other ponies.

The cat does not like to get wet.

She also does not like to do chores.

But there is nothing she hates more than when someone tries to steal her toys!

It is not just the ponies of Ponyville
who have pets.

Princess Celestia has a phoenix
named Philomena.

Philomena has a special talent.

She can burst into flames!

Philomena sometimes uses that
talent to play tricks on the ponies.
Fluttershy has never seen
anything like it!

Even Spike has a pet.

Peewee is a baby phoenix.

Spike rescued Peewee back
when he was still an egg.

Pets are hard work!

But the ponies love them.

And the pets love the ponies!

Because friendship is magic, and
pets are a very special kind of friend!